AFTER TEN THOUSAND YEARS, DESIRE

FRANÇOIS CHARRON

After Ten Thousand Years, Desire:
Selected Recent Poems

TRANSLATED BY
Bruce Whiteman
and
Francis Farley-Chevrier

Toronto: ECW PRESS, 1995

Permission to prepare and publish these translations was
kindly granted by François Hébert of Les Herbes Rouges.

CANADIAN CATALOGUING IN PUBLICATION DATA

Charron, François, 1952-
After ten thousand years, desire : selected recent poems

Poems
ISBN 1-55022-224-4

I. Whiteman, Bruce, 1952- . II. Farley-Chevrier,
Francis, 1973- . III. Title.

PS8555.H36A74 1995   C841'.54   C95-930910-1
PQ3919.2.C53A74 1995

Published with the financial assistance of
The Canada Council and the Ontario Arts Council

Cover photograph by Carlo Cantini.
Set in Monotype Poliphilus and Blado
by ECW Type & Art, Oakville, Ontario.
Printed by Métropole Litho, Sherbrooke, Quebec.

Published by ECW PRESS, 2120 Queen Street East,
Suite 200, Toronto, Ontario, Canada M4E 1E2.

TABLE OF CONTENTS

For the Lovers (1992)

INTRODUCTION

"La poésie et la pensée devraient, pour moi, toujours coïncider. (Cette note devrait plaire à François Charron.)"
— André Roy, *La Vie parallèle: Un carnet* (1994)

Although his work is little known in English Canada, in Quebec, François Charron is one of the best-known poets of his generation. Born in 1952 in Longueuil, south across the river from Montreal, he has long been associated with the avantgarde writers who published in the magazines *Les Herbes rouges* (which evolved into a publishing house of the same name) and *La nouvelle barre du jour*: Claude Beausoleil, Normand de Bellefeuille, Roger Des Roches, André Roy, and others.

Charron began to write as a teenager, and eventually he became one of the most prolific of the Herbes rouges poets. His first writing was dense and highly colloquial, including for example an early (and largely untranslatable) series of parodies and literary nose-thumbings called *Littérature/obscenités* (1974). A sociopolitical dedication was evident in his poetry then, in common with much of the work of the younger experimental Quebec writers of the 1970s. "I wanted to create texts," he remarked in an interview in 1991, "which could be seen as progres-sive, which would run parallel to the most avantgarde social movements."* Charron would work his way through several phases after his juvenilia, including some formalist, theory-oriented writing (*Blessures*, which won the Le Prix Émile-Nelligan in 1979) before arriving at the simpler, more personal style which characterizes most of the second half of this book.

The evolution towards a quasi-oriental spiritual simplicity in Char-ron's work has not been a direct one. He has never confined himself stylistically, and with every two or three books has seemed to change direction. "I am not a completed idea," as he says in a poem published

---

* "Et je voulais faire des textes qui se situent dans la ligne du progrès, qui avancent en parallèle avec les mouvements sociaux les plus d'avantgarde." Pierre Ouellet et Jacques Pelletier, "Écrire le réel: Entretien avec François Charron," *Voix & images* 16, 3 (printemps 1991), p. 382.

in *L'Intraduisible Amour* (1991), "I walk slowly at the edge of the road."* Partly for this reason, reviewers have not always found him easy to deal with, and his work has attracted commentary that ranges from the openly dismissive to the encomiastic. His poetry has nevertheless received many awards, among them Le Prix Canada-Belgique (1983), Le Grand prix de poésie de la Fondation Les Forges (1990), Le Prix Air-Canada (1991), Le Grand prix de poésie du Journal de Montréal (1992), and no less than four Governor-General's award nominations, in addition to Le Prix Nelligan already mentioned. In the words of Jean Royer, Charron "has become one of the richest inheritors of Quebec poetry."**

The poems in this book have been selected from five of Charron's books published over the last ten years. The collection falls into two roughly equal halves, the first consisting of work from *La Vie n'a pas de sens* (1985), *Le Fait de vivre ou d'avoir vécu* (1986), and *La Fragilité des choses* (1987), and the second of selections from *La beauté pourrit sans douleur* (1989), and *Pour les amants* (1992). The work in the first half embodies certain metaphysical concerns carried forward from earlier Charron books, though the beginnings of a greater simplicity of expression are apparent here, particularly in *La Fragilité des choses*:

> The city in love is full of unknown people
> at rest. They go to sit down, read
> to each other, sketch countries with
> profound laws, houses that meditate.
> At night, full of strangers, the city
> becomes full of possibility. And I stay there,
> at ease, in a place still open,
> always with something new to
> talk about and discover a city.

---

* François Charron, "Acceuil," in *L'Intraduisible amour* (Trois-Rivières: Écrits des forges, 1991), p. 139.

** "Charron est devenu un des plus riches héritiers de la poésie québécoise." Jean Royer, *Introduction à la poésie québécoise* (Montreal: Bibliothèque québécoise, 1989), p. 169.

An increasing emphasis on the concrete and the quotidian runs in parallel with the greater importance of love as the central subject and the medium of transcendence ("the ghost/at your nape is an infinite being/who takes care of you").

With *La Beauté pourrit sans douleur* Charron's poetry arrives fully at that will to simplification ("la volonté de simplification") remarked by Ouellet and Pelletier in the *Voix & images* interview. This and the following collection demonstrate a radical paring down (a purification, he calls it) of Charron's language, a growing reliance on a perceptual and expressive parataxis that will remind English-Canadian readers of Imagist practice, though Charron is more willing to interweave the subjective with the enumerative statement than was William Carlos Williams or W.W.E. Ross or Raymond Souster. In *La Beauté pourrit sans douleur* this mix of the inner and the outer is rather carefully controlled by an almost haiku-like austerity of form. With *Pour les amants*, however, Charron returns to the prose poem for the first time since a book called simply *François* (1984), and here one feels that his spiritual simplicities have found their true form. These are lovely poems of often pure state-ment that nevertheless have a wonderful erotic aura:

> I'd like to be alone. Once again time has passed. A woman has opened her red umbrella. A first truck goes past on the road. In a bistro the chairs are being put up on the tables. The situation changes easily. Taking a step back from everything, I relinquish a version of the earth that is too familiar. I know that we will be only a memory, an act of waiting at the end of a lane, and my task is to forget.

"Une femme a ouvert son parapluie rouge" is simple enough as an observation, but Charron manages to suggest so much beyond the literal as well, beginning with the irony of a now unforgettable act caught forever in a poem entitled "Oublier."

François Charron is only in mid-career, and his work to date — its variety as well as its prolificity — makes it likely that future books will go off in directions unpredictible on the basis of *Pour les amants* and his most recent book, *Clair génie du vent*, published in 1994. We hope that these translations will help to make Charron's work better known to English-speaking readers in Canada and elsewhere.

Tant qu'il y aura des vocables, nous les prononcerons pour apprivoiser la pure lumière de la mort. ("Parlez de soi")

As long as there are words, we will voice them to tame the pure light of death. ("Talking About Oneself")

Bruce Whiteman & Francis Farley-Chevrier
February 1995

La Vie n'a pas de sens

Life Doesn't Make Sense (1985)

from *Everywhere and Never*

Let me tell you, time begins at night.
Wait a little longer and it's too late,
Night turns over and drowns in the sea,
And without night, the hands are condemned to
All the doors and roads
We never hear about.
Let me tell you about the voice outside which
Shows me each voice, restrained, rejected,
Long whispers the water makes on the windows,
Thinking about you afterwards on the grass
After someone has died.

Our body is now a memory without a
Window. It's not worth running,
Space rises up on its own to
Touch us faintly, space carries memory along
With the scary swiftness of an airplane.
And for a moment the heart (that hoary old word)
Rises again through our hunger and thirst,
The heart strays over the roofs of cities,
Its limits are impossible to imagine.
Life can wait no longer, life is
Utterly life.

We touch the silence each time to make
The silence fall. We didn't hear,
We remained at the corner of the table
With a cigarette burning down.
Talk takes us in, talk dresses the wounds
On our hands and feet, while far away the
Riverbanks support our birth which is invented,
Asserted, constantly snatched from the old
Images which sentences evoke.
At this moment what we have made
Is reduced to this edge, this space of
Time licked by quick breaths. No one
Will come to take back the black contour
Of our mouth (undivided measure).

The book exists usually without
Lending depth to the face. At the end of a street, at
The end of a door I see my own eyes, I see the
Surface of my eyes, then the first sign, obstinately,
That opens on the secret spaces of the book.
Suns and clouds dive into its law,
Into the strength of its law and the fear of
Losing it. Where is it going? What does it undo?
It is a huge question, repeated again and again at
Each step. Everywhere and never the earth
Would like simply to crack its enigma.
I quote (or would like to) the drama of the faraway
Look of dirty water, of sperm or blood,
Everywhere and never.

Once again the manuscript turned over.
It disappeared behind the furniture, under
Objects, through the curtains. Its evidence
Leaves us, its evidence fades, and only the
Burn marks scattered untidily on the
Floor of the room survive. Against all logic
We are spectators here in this ruin, second
By second — nails that are driven
Through each of our fingers. An era
(A gesture) brings us to state it:
Fragile rampart, rotted castle, stunning
Beauty that demands we find
A lasting example or noise.

from *There Is No More Light*

It happened with my fists scattered to the
Four winds, without suspecting that I was getting to the heart
Of the too pale mausoleum. I was giving my flattened forehead,
My forehead overcome by the middle and the end
(Remember the middle and the end). I was like a
Blind man whose steps are no longer on the ground.
It happened before me, the generations before me,
The description of what the river in front of me
Looks like. The river hung by a thread, and
I called out to you, you, in the feeling I
Had of you, of your island, of your sleep, of
Your breasts. I made a path to
Regain the pose left vacant. What
Deprives us, what preserves us: we can't
Talk about it (or how to talk about it?).
Physical clarity is irrepressible.

How will that come? How will you manage to
Gather the incantations, then launch them like
A boat is launched, like a boat is
Unlashed? You intelligent people, tell me whether
The spells are abolished or the cantatas resound,
Whether the forbidden photographs descend on the
Public places. You, in the unpartitioning of the
Sky, with your hair, with your napes, tell me about
The directions taken by the rays of the strong
Light. When something stops striking us,
There is no more heat, there is no more light.

Why so restless, why this departure, these great
Marks spread over the stitch of numbers?
Why this migration behind the ear
When I am unborn and when the ancient
Panoplies are violently consumed? I act,
I drip, I cry out the lake of my body.
The evening is too high, the metaphor too
White, the diary of my signatures comes to me
To solve that. I only have to admit it,
However unexpected it is. From whom? For when?
In what? Which way? Closer up, a needle
Astonishes the spectacle of the world.

I claim the wheel, its inexistence that takes our measure.
I claim chance which never looks the same
Twice. I claim the groaning of labyrinths
Without caring about labyrinths. The knots
Come to us, their swaying rocks us,
Their answers sneak out between two lips.
(What do you expect us to be told?) I claim
Joys branching and spreading out over all
The breadth of our tissues. I claim billboards
That are warped, that fail to belong to
What they find. Impossible to betray the
Poem. I love what I love. So it is, just
As it is (the message is read as it is).

Where you stretch out there is inevitably
Something. The idleness of our acts undoes
The edges of the room. This: the room. This:
The edges. This: the acts. We turn around.
We change places. Clarity rests in the hope
Of mirrors. If it moves, the vision is inhaled
Or disturbed, it cannot sleep. We pass a
Rag, we pull on a bit of string, everything
That will live melds with the earth: organs,
Small change, theorems, *unthinkable decay*.
Pillars cleared out, we gain access to our fears
And our century. The century personifies
Inexhaustible truth. There is definitely
Something.

Le Fait de vivre ou d'avoir vécu

The Fact of Living or of Having Lived (1986)

The Patience of Disaster

I

The disaster of our bellies is patient
and blind, it belongs to the invisible
works of slowness (a fire
lights up the slow constellation of the
works). The human person
subsequently wraps himself up inside a
blanket, stretches out on the
tile floor, lives amidst bits of paper,
envelopes, pieces of string.
The human person goes almost
unnoticed. The disaster of our bellies
orbits a blasted planet.
Undecipherable permanence of the real.

I I

There was nothing, perpetual motion
informs the lungs, prepares to
replace the day with the day on
our upright legs. Hallways run
out, defeat retranslates the
outline of closets and chests.
Always close by, always permeable,
the victim relentlessly repeats
the same punishment. His back is turned.
His coat is not far off.

III

Somewhere below, the earth
caresses the marks we offer it
and that disaster turns inside out.
The latter is set beside a black pool
(black as murder is black).
Almost directly, almost completely
it forces beauty to be
endlessly swallowed up then destroyed.
Disaster will never have been ours,
and we will never have known what it
was.

I V

Thus the cliff breaks apart
to become untouchable (our
hands are amazed that they no longer know how to
touch). The depthless square,
lacking density, stays buried in
the grass, and our hands go
oddly astray, are abolished, seem
never to have been. We will judge,
we will prescribe, skimming over
the square flat in the grass. This
memory is hard to imagine.

V

Though we cease to call it up,
memory surfaces all the same.
The rectangular room . . . the strangely
wavy atmosphere . . . We can feel the rain
that swells to blend with
the walls of the room. The square
in a corner of the room (or floating
over the grass) represents something
for someone. It rots, sways,
stops moving. The paradox lasts only
a few seconds. The person is
at a loss.

V I

To move about inside
apartments, to be almost
sure of it, we must assume
this relation to the inverting body,
this relation to signs from the outside.
Sexes . . . values . . . nothingness.
The patience of disaster leaves us
solitary beside a cup, beside
water, beside the dissolving
cup and water. Being
trembles one last time; again it
closes the notebook of disaster.

Waste, Desires

I

In the underground room (becoming
still) noises settle down to
work. The mirror does not get
bored, the mirror is always there as
things happen: projections,
uneven parts, the ceiling.
Today anyone arrives
exactly in the (still) room
to crawl along the floor
to the crack in the corner.
Desire — what it does and
why — is a large pale
compartment, latticed, which tells us
neither when nor how a gesture gets through,
curves in, is laid from top to bottom
on a surface.

I I

Infused in this room (there is
no other way) our own suffering
leads us to the flesh's intensity,
to spasms, to sweat, to slaver
scratching the line of the shield.
The shroud, stained with ink,
unused, stinking, grows
lustreless and perceptibly like
the dull flatness of the wall. The wall is
there because it's there, along with the
thin film of desire, like sulphur, like
straw. The wall remains there all
day.

III

Our unspoken agreements already escape
through the cover. The thick cover,
woven and subtly ornamented,
falls on us, enshrouds what
we hold close to our hearts. No
formula simplifies this cover.
Neither its weight nor its length
nor its width succeeds in
lodging itself in memory. Someone's emotion
will come later to waste what it
might have wanted to hang on to.
Knives invoked, garbage called on
to slash the thickness of the
cover.

IV

What we leave unsaid festers
at the end of the third day; festers with
the rings, with griefs, festers
freely, chained to the board which has been
bitten and scratched. The dense mass
of what we leave unsaid vibrates
like a film in which the listener
visualizes his desertions. The listener
(at the end of the third day) is discretely
resurrected. He does so because at
the same time he perceives the
neutrality of the neuter.

V

This is the only point of view,
the sole photograph, worn almost,
now deprived of light. We
imagine trains, postcards,
the desertion of evening.
How odd it is . . . We imagine
the bottom of a valley, unexpected
tremors, immense pieces of
paper, the black and shiny stars
that Mozart in agony put at the head
of his bed. The saliva spread
on our fingers, on our eyelids, thinks about
the resemblance which does not exist.

VI

At the end of a fit length of time,
not a single word had yet been spoken.
Destiny — taken down, washed again,
folded in two in a notebook — remains still.
It is closer, it is higher.
Here and there desire comes to grief
inside us, centres around the
iris; our habitual actions
continue without making any claims.
Desire — that laughable yet
dreadful thing — seeks
entrance to our very soul.
The resemblance as such might
once have made itself known.

You

I

Me in front of you, I will feel,
I will think, I will write, and all of this
will reach you gliding near by.
What is me against a table of such
and such a height, what is me
between the right and left hands
will go on despite what
we hold back; and me before
you I will know that the ghost
at your nape is an infinite being
who takes care of you.

II

Delicately we will approach the blue
thread, the strap hidden under
the pillow, a little as though it should
have another coherence, a different
acknowledgement in the manner of
signing a treaty. You and I,
this takes place anywhere once.
This could never have called
on us. It would have been too late
or too early, we would not have noticed
anything. Someone would have finished
by saying: "I think I will go
home." It would have been a very
simple story like so many.

La Fragilité des choses

The Fragility of Things (1987)

The Ability to Change Places

Children roam about in the open air. They
are amazed at the music that grazes
their temples, they marvel at a barricade,
they gaze at a sheet floating along a
wall. Children break apart nature's
operations, their perceptions are scattered,
their feelings are always already lost.
The fragmented nature of a child's
perceptions avoids the last word and changes
places again (the more I write, the more I
find we must change places).

The Stillness of a Curtain Along a Wall

At night I move about with huge eyes.
The darkness makes no claims. The world happens.
A doorway leads me to the heart of the city.
Near a sidewalk, a curtain along a wall
remains still. The events which do not occur
inhabit an extinct and solitary forest.
That night a stranger agrees to
meet me. Night draws near, it
occupies the whole earth. It's always the
same image of night, it's always the
same close tear.

The First Movement Is the Only Movement

A single movement is enough to enter
somewhere. Today I have lunch at
one o'clock. In the afternoon I'll work
at home or take a certain stree´ again
to talk to a friend in a café. Sometimes
I take the newspaper in my hands.
I have no taste left for argument or for
carrying out work. Passers-by along
the sidewalks follow one another without
acknowledgement. Most often
past experience strikes me as already half-
buried. (One experience sheds light on
another experience, but Man's destiny
is outside all experience.
In the end, nothing could be saved.)

The Obstacle Is Inseparable From Time

We are afraid to wander and to face
the outside. We would like to avoid mistakes,
we would like to eliminate something which might be
a mistake. Scattered pieces are still
visible despite the dim light. The
same sighs form on the surface of
lips. The universe is alone, absolutely alone,
perfectly alone. A soiled photograph
lies against the floor, dust
settles on the floor. We don't consider
where we walk anymore. Or how.
Or why. After a certain point,
the obstacle is no longer something
natural.

Something Very Calm

The city often falls in love with its
people. Every day I am somewhere else in
the city that loves us, and in spite of myself,
the imponderable opens a way for me through
the city's quarters. The imponderable breaks up
conventionalities and lets me go everywhere slowly.
I barely move, and when I let go and
feel myself breathe, all difficulties
evaporate in an infinitely truthful reality.
The city in love is full of unknown people
at rest. They go to sit down, read
to each other, sketch countries with
profound laws, houses that meditate.
At night, full of strangers, the city
becomes full of possibility. And I stay there,
at ease, in a place still open,
always with something new to
talk about and discover a city.

The Lie Licks Our Eyes

The lie restricts space because it
can no longer call and live in space.
From time to time my conscience
perceives the lie that licks our eyes;
it then lets happiness impregnate some
part of our eyes, and happiness in
our eyes lets us meet here again at
once. So I remember that I embrace
oblivion, that this proof of oblivion persists
inexplicably, that my spirit perishes
there each time. The lie which came
or may come suddenly falters in front of me.
The lie in the middle of space has no
real place and I have to acknowledge that
deep down we are blinded by it. I'm the
living one who, having felt this, stands up.

Our Clothes Beneath the Rain

We have not yet paid attention
to our clothes beneath the rain (the colours
of our clothes change beneath the rain).
The edges of the rain hear our steps
coming and our words resound in our steps.
This confidence escaped a beginning,
this confidence gives itself fearlessly to an
extreme emotion. Now the water flows
and washes down and thins out; it is diffused
very gently. The rainwater which comes
fills me with tenderness. It wets my
silent cheeks, it puts me face to face with
something larger than myself. The rain⁄
water that comes, comes close to
no one and is ignorant of itself.

Earth and Dream

The dreamer goes forward over all necessities.
The sleeping bridges puzzle him, the light
moves without him, at the close of day he swims
beneath the sea. Most of the time somewhere
he holds a book and goes off without
reassuring us. Echoes will certainly grow
weaker, fascination will leave us.
Still, on a street corner, the sweet dreamer,
impassive, says hello to the first
person he runs into. He breaks the sound
barrier, he listens in in the passageways
where unavowed farewells glide by. The word
leaving (but it's not wanted) suddenly
prevents the set from closing up again.

A Black Line

Our prophesying consummates secrets,
embraces, conflicts in which buildings
shake. It knows that every gesture
of ours flies off on a voyage and returns
like the sun around the earth.
Behind me, behind my face lit up,
the great opacity rages, and the separation
from the great opacity makes each
of my gestures return like the sun
around the earth. Thus I bare a
black line in the cavity of my mouth, on
the whole area of my mouth. The prophecies are
finally brought together, search out the
smallest places and come to get me.
Silence remembers my thoughts.

The Speaker's Hand

Who still speaks through the torments?
Who tries to recover that missing base
supposed by fear? The speaker's
hand has remained free forever. It admires
movement become absence, it soothes
the wanderers on the road, it sneaks in
among the ships paralyzed like dry
wood. Each scene of our present life allows
air to circulate between word and body.
Torments capture us from afar, they
set us down in fragility. We fall silent,
we have no more strength. Our
vision withers . . . We look out on a
gentle snow at the end of a hard day . . .
We are seen and get by on what will
never have been.

Whither Truth?

Truth betrays us when it no longer wants
to break away. But where can it go,
truth? Under a streetlight truth is
a pale clarity, a loss of memory,
something that does not hold on to what is.
Beings who demand to love each other join
forces, climb onto ladders,
build platforms, set off to
look for an ancient formula,
a formula misunderstood or misapplied,
a formula learned to keep us from fear
against our will. On the same sidewalk
stand all those who wonder what they
did with truth, and they open their
hands, and they close their hands, and
the freshness of the air lets them
love one another again.

La Beauté pourrit sans douleur

Beauty Rots Without Pain (1989)

Things We Cannot Say

all those things we cannot say
the wan moon behind the clouds
the transparency of the seasons
the water at your lips
the light on your skin
we let this grow
later the pure sound of the air

but something else again
a hand on my shoulder
our breath in the cold
the pattern on your dress
the sun seems smaller and I want nothing to drink
it's not that yet

life is too beautiful
life is too clear
there are howlings of birds
the land touches the sea
dawn breaks a little earlier
we see nothing and must return with an empty heart

open shutters
the light in the centre of the room
a map of the world fills the wall
various objects are found again
leaves hover in the sky
after ten thousand years, desire

there is the breathing of this woman
I feel it near my eyes
I feel it separated from my eyes
our past doesn't hear us anymore
sweat runs down the back
we weigh what the day leaves us
the immensity of the day is beyond compare

I let the cold water tap run
a radio comes on
we get caught by noises
you are wearing a summer dress
the language is nowhere within us
the outside is nowhere within us
the drapes begin to move
you forgot your gloves somewhere
soon we won't think about it anymore

you lower your eyelids
my bedroom is aired out
a jug breaks
I turn the pages of a book
swallows fly up and down
you keep uneasiness from me
you put your head on my lap
we remain in space heat at our fingertips

I pick up a scarf
the blinds rattle in the wind
the floors get dirty
you call me often
at night the moon lights up our clothes
at night our clothes smell good
you invent a new way of smiling

I'll go to see you tomorrow
glasses lie on the sofa
an hypothesis is no longer valid
someone gets up again
someone wants to live with someone
an umbrella stays wide open
who will remember an existence?

Death Gives Us the Habit of Speech

the fingers move
I'm invited to stay
death gives us the habit of speech

     *

knowledge is already wounded
some ashes remain, some passengers leave again
clear water keeps us from a second life

     *

a pile of leaves at the edge of a roof
passers-by who do not open their mouths
I set up a swing in the middle of the day

     *

two triangles look alike
a girlfriend had the time to greet me
we are alone within moments

     *

this suitcase is tightly closed
I am sitting somewhere
a cloud will not descend a second time

     *

I'm looking for words in the rain
little by little languour makes itself felt
I take a long walk at the edge of the fields

*

the mountain does not want to leave
we let ourselves be caught off guard
the sounds of childhood burn in dream

*

I think about those who save their money
a lamp goes out in the forest
a neighbour asks me where I live

*

a little girl throws a stone
an angel stands still
lovers on a streetcorner hug each other tightly
*

I move a piece of furniture to make room for myself
a dying feeling is a very strange thing
sometimes we don't know how to do without something in the way

*

snowflakes disappear on contact with the street
not to believe anyone remains an indescribable event
chance makes me see my face in a mirror

*

distance listens to us and the earth ages
a voice speaks in my ear
we will tire without leaving the patience of the roadways

Everything Became Simple

it is noon, we take this narrow street
you press your feet against the damp pavement
you give your eyes to the radiance of the landscape
forms move, forms brush against us and grow dim
people stand before their doors
slowly our thoughts scatter in the middle of the street
it is always noon, we won't drink at once
our thoughts seem much freer when we watch them

here is the last house
I hear bottles clinking
smoke from the chimneys foretells the breeze
we progress by letting the innocence of things come to us
we breathe to swallow a moment of this sky
I let a match flare
the icy lake water is repeated at each moment
everywhere happiness continues to be at hand

you give me a glass of wine
we don't know what time it is
we take two cushions to lie down on
the indifferent ground, the smell of the storm, the air
  turns colder than the water
we let some of our ideas fade away
on the window sill a bottle is half-full

I drop a knife on the ground
for a few seconds no one moves
a clock does not work
you come near my gaze
the meaning grows larger, shutters are half-opened
the sun heats a white plate on the edge of the table

the week which is starting is nothing special
the smell of fall steals calmly upon us
I put on a navy blue sweater
we leave the house to celebrate at the restaurant
an aspen leaf whirls about briefly before sticking in the mud
later the sun sets
it is pointless to say or to think up anything else

you talk to me about old wounds
you question the fear of dying under the leaves turned almost red
many graffiti appear on the walls
I think of the cold that we pick up crossing the yard
lights blink, my soul is at the end of the street
I admire the puddles along the sidewalks
you press against me, and say *I am happy*
there is a new infinity on your face, and it is yourself

it's very dark in the kitchen, I don't utter a word
I go outside to check the temperature
the days are getting shorter, the days are wrapped in silence
a door closes by itself
what is us this first of December has not been translated
what is us today ends with a little laziness

you lean your head here precisely
deep in the black air your pupils still shine
elsewhere a neon sign lights up a shop window
three minutes go by, you take hold of my neck
it's Sunday night, the snow cuts us off
we have lost all track of time, the mountain of memories is as
   light as a feather

you draw something on cardboard
a border is rebuilt
life goes on, we really want it to
we could believe that time acts like a father

your mouth in the waning winter light, your mouth alive against all odds
we hear the rumbling of traffic, your silhouette is outlined next to mine
far off clouds like dreams embrace the abyss
tomorrow in the same place we will know thirst again

Pour les amants

For the Lovers (1992)

The sky desires the earth, the sky is a stone at the tips of my fingers. I lift my head, the day is naked. I tell you that you are beautiful, that your face is soft, inexhaustible. The world which remains open has forgotten that we are here. Behind the mist, the stateless mountains sketch an eternal memory.

Tomorrow

The dazzling disk of the moon distracts us for a moment. The evening growing deeper slips between the roofs. A cat scarcely dares to creep forward. The earth turns in the midst of a dream, we can say "I" without aim or intention. You whispered a phrase to me looking straight into my eyes. We hear a train pass in the distance, the surge lifts up your hair, a streetlight buzzes. Everything looks much closer to us than usual. Wanting each other, tomorrow is an absence of the purest white.

To Forget

I'd like to be alone. Once again time has passed. A woman has opened her red umbrella, a first truck goes past on the road. In a bistro the chairs are being put up on the tables. The situation changes easily. Taking a step back from everything, I relinquish a version of the earth that is too familiar. I know that we will be only a memory, an act of waiting at the end of a lane, and my task will be to forget.

Loving Is a Mystery

My eyelids close softly beneath your lips, self-renunciation makes us alive. What matters here is faceless now. Loving is a mystery fed by the flames. The certainty of being alive leaves the door open. We enjoy ourselves, at ease beneath the sun, we drink the fluidity of silence together. Bewitched, our awareness finds itself grown larger.

Words themselves listen to words. I am not afraid to be wrong. I go further than myself. The voice touches what must be found, the centre speaks of absence. I go off so that emptiness may take my place. Dying passes through my mouth, everything that exists is happening this instant.

Self-Discovery

Writing is a silence we might have lost. The events remain undecided among the stones. A world always the same falls back into gentleness or hatred. The truth does not hinder us from being alone. Time is a super-illusion. To be right is worth nothing. We ourselves are a limitless invention. There is no need to demonstrate anything.

The Gift of Emotion

There is the day of our birth, there is the day of our death. Everyone makes a lot of fuss about tomorrow. A star come from the confines has given us back the gift of emotion, the universe explores our blood. I am an impression which gives in to the end that is there. I shall continue to grow old so as to perfect my childhood.

Fire and wind give rise to blind words. The guiding conscience contains legends. An act of love given freely passes gently through us and glorifies our bodies. The invention of the past is immediate. I labour alone in the darkness, I try not to think. Wanting too hard to seize the why of things, the depths of the person become a shadow.

I hear the essential emptiness of first meeting and farewell resonate within me, every fault at last looks possible. Talking about yourself is to affirm an alien certainty. To think about what is continuously break-ing loose is to wake up. As long as there are words, we will voice them to tame the pure light of death.

Receiving

Breath of the stars . . . Charity of wide spaces . . . I have worked as far from myself as possible. In my thinking I have been increasingly aware of the seconds, the years, the centuries, and the untranslatable starts up beneath each of my steps. I have written this book to release myself from beginnings and predictible endings, I have written this book for the lovers who create miracles. Where at last we no longer know what must be, there the most vivid emotion enters into us, to receive us.

Books By François Charron

18 assauts (1972)

Au «sujet» de la poésie (1972)

Projet d'écriture pour l'été 76 (1973)

La Traversée/le regard (under the name André Lamarre) (1973)

Littérature/obscénités (1974)

Persister et se maintenir dans les vertiges de la terre qui demeurent sans fin (1974)

Interventions politiques (1975)

Pirouette par hasard poésie (1975)

Enthousiasme (1976)

Du commencement à la fin (1977)

Propagande (1977)

Feu [preceded by] *Langue(s)* 1978

Blessures (1978)

Peinture automatiste [preceded by] *Qui parle dans la théorie?* (1979)

Le Temps échappé des yeux: Notes sur l'expérience de la peinture (1979)

1980 (1981)

Mystère (1981)

La Passion d'autonomie: Littérature et nationalisme (1982)

Toute parole m'éblouira (1982)

D'où viennent les tableaux? (1983)

Je suis ce que je suis (1983)

François (1984)

Le Fait de vivre ou d'avoir vécu (1986)

Le Monde comme obstacle (1988)

La Beauté pourrit sans douleur [with] *La Très précieuse qualité du vide* (1989)

La Beauté des visages ne pèse pas sur la terre (1990)

L'Intraduisible amour (1991)

Pour les amants (1992)

La Vie n'a pas de sens [with] *La Chambre des miracles*
     [and] *La Fragilité des choses* (1993)

Clair génie du vent (1994)